Kim and Sal were in the
shed in Polly's garden.
A chest was in the corner.

"There are tricks in
that chest," said Kim.

"I like tricks," said Sal.

There was a trick mug
in the chest.
"This mug drips when you
pick it up," said Kim.

"Cool!" said Sal. "Let's have some fun. Let's trick Polly. She will get so wet!"

Kim put some milk in the trick mug. Then he put some milk in Sal's mug.

11

They took the
mugs to Polly.
"Have some milk,
Polly," said Kim.

"Thank you!" said Polly.
"I like milk, but can
you get me a snack
as well?"

Kim and Sal
went to get
a snack.

Then Polly took the mug.
She drank some milk.
But the mug did not drip.

Kim and Sal were cross!

Sal took her mug.
She drank some milk.
Drip! Drip! Drip!

"What a mess, Sal!" said Kim.

"Got you!" said Polly.
"*That* is the trick mug!"

Puzzles

Match the words that rhyme to the pictures!

brick

best

trick

test

milk

boss

silk

Tricks

chest

flick

toss

stick

cross

vest

Answers

trick – brick, flick, stick

chest – best, test, vest

milk – silk

cross – boss, toss

Espresso Connections

This book may be used in conjunction with the Literacy area on Espresso to secure children's phonics learning. Here are some suggestions.

Word Machine
Encourage children to play the Word Machine Level 2. Demonstrate how the machine works, and then move on to the activities.

Ask children to find the correct beginnings. Then ask children to find the correct endings.

Check that children are able to hear the difference between the letter sounds as different words come up.

Praise plausible attempts, such as substituting the letter "k" for "c" when attempting to find the hard c sound.

Spot the Word
Choose a book from the Big Book selection to play Spot the Word.

Give children pieces of paper with the high frequency words said, so, have, like, some, come, were, there, little, one, do, when, out or what. (The class could be split, with groups of children looking for different words.)

Ask children to note down on the paper each time they have seen or heard the word they are looking for.

At the end of the book, children should count up how many times their target word has been used.

Go back through the book together and see whether they got it right.

Praise plausible attempts, for example "live" for "like" and take the opportunity to point out why these words are different.

You could replicate the activity with this phonics story.